Dear Parents,

ASPCA® Rescue Readers series tells stories of animal adventures from the animal's point of view! Written with warmth and gentle humor, these leveled texts are designed to support young readers in their growth while connecting to their passion for pets.

Level 2 in this series is designed for early readers who need short, simple sentences, familiar vocabulary, informative illustrations, and easier spelling patterns to give them support as they practice to become fluent readers.

When you're reading with your children, you can help by encouraging them to think about using more than one strategy to unlock new words. Successful readers solve words in a variety of ways. Here are some tips you might share with your child:

- Take a picture walk before you read so you can preview the story.

- Sound out the words, remembering that some letters say more than one sound.

- For long words, cover up the end so you can figure out the beginning first.

- Check the picture to see if it gives you some clues.

- Skip over a word and read a little further along. Then come back to it.

- Think about what is happening in this story. What would make sense here?

Learning to read is an exciting time in a child's life. A wonderful way to share in that time is to have conversations about the books after reading. Children love talking about their favorite part, or connecting the story to their own lives. I hope you'll enjoy sharing in the fun as your children get to know Nibbles and all the other adopted pets that are part of this series. Happy reading!

Ellie Costa, M.S. Ed.
Literacy Specialist, Bank Street College of Education

Published by Studio Fun International, Inc.
44 South Broadway, White Plains, NY 10601 U.S.A. and
Studio Fun International Limited,
The Ice House, 124-126 Walcot Street, Bath UK BA1 5BG
Illustration © 2015 Studio Fun International, Inc.
Text © 2015 ASPCA®
Studio Fun Books is a trademark of Studio Fun International, Inc.,
a subsidiary of The Reader's Digest Association, Inc.
Printed in China.
Conforms to ASTM F963
10 9 8 7 6 5 4 3 2 1
SL2/03/15
Cover guinea pig photos © inkwelldodo/shutterstock.com

***The American Society for the Prevention of Cruelty to Animals (ASPCA®) will
receive a minimum guarantee from Studio Fun International, Inc. of $25,000
for the sale of ASPCA® products through December 2017.
Comments? Questions? Call us at: 1-800-217-3346**

Library of Congress Cataloging-in-Publication Data

Froeb, Lori.
  I am Nibbles / Lori Froeb ; illustrated by Tammie Lyon.
      pages cm. -- (Rescue readers ; 3)
  Summary: "Meet Nibbles the guinea pig. When a kid named Zack brings Nibbles home over vacation,
he learns just how the guinea pig got his name!"-- Provided by publisher.
  ISBN 978-0-7944-3455-7 (paperback) -- ISBN 978-0-7944-3456-4 (hard cover)
  1. Hamsters--Juvenile fiction. [1. Hamsters--Fiction.] I. Title.
  PZ10.3.F9335Iaq 2015
  [E]--dc23
                              2015002709

I Am Nibbles

written by
Nibbles

(with help from Lori C. Froeb)

illustrated by Tammie Lyon

studio fun BOOKS

White Plains, New York • Montréal, Québec • Bath, United Kingdom

Hi there!

I am Nibbles.

I am always hungry!

I belong to Miss Kate.
She is a teacher.
This is her classroom.
I am the class pet.

You can see why my name is Nibbles.

The classroom
has lots of things to chew.
I try them all.

I nibble the art.

I nibble the plants.

Once I nibbled a kid's shirt.
That was an accident.

I am going on a trip.
School is closed for vacation.
I can go home with Zack.
I can't wait!

"Watch out for Nibbles!" says Miss Kate.

"He nibbles!"

I think that's funny.

Miss Kate knows me very well!

Zack will keep me in his room.

I see a lot of new things to nibble!

Zack has a baby sister.
Zack's sister likes to nibble too!
That toy looks nice and sweet.

I want to see more of Zack's house.
When he gives me food and water,
I will try to run past him!

Quick!
Up the ladder!

Trapped!
Zack is too fast.

I have another chance to escape!
Zack is cleaning my cage.
This box is easy to nibble!
Nibble, nibble, nibble.
Soon I will be free.
Look out! Here I come!

14

15

Where should I go first?

No one sees me. I am fast!

There is a book on the floor.
It is a book about me!

I nibble through it.
It tastes just like the box!

Uh-oh. I hear Zack.

He is looking for me.

But I am not done exploring.

18

This white stuff is easy to nibble!
There is more and more.
I like this mess!

Look at all the animals.
When Zack comes in
I hide in the middle.

He looks at me, but he can't see me.

I nibble a fuzzy bear.

Yuck! The fuzz sticks in my teeth.

There is so much to nibble.

I try some homework...

...a drumstick...

...a shoe...

The shoe is stinky.

Uh-oh. Zack is coming.

I need to hide.

I smell something yummy.

This is a good place to hide.

Nibble, nibble, nibble.

My nibbling gives me away.
Zack opens the pack...

...and finds me.

"You are a rascal, Nibbles!" Zack says.
It feels good when he pets my fur.

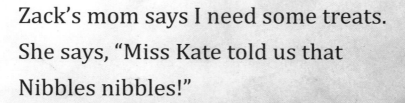

Zack's mom says I need some treats.
She says, "Miss Kate told us that
Nibbles nibbles!"

Look what I have in my cage now.
Yummy carrots! Celery! Alfalfa!
There is an apple for dessert.

Life is sweet.

Zack is my new favorite kid.

It's good to be back in the classroom.
There are always new things to nibble.

Zack put a new sign near my home.
I think I'll have a bite right now.

Caring for Guinea Pigs

Guinea pigs make great pets and are not difficult to care for. Here are some basic tips.

- Use a large cage with a solid bottom. The larger the cage, the better. Each guinea pig should have at least four square feet of space.

- Line the bottom of the cage with bedding (hardwood shavings or processed paper).

- Change the soiled bedding every day and wash the cage once a week with warm water and soap.

- Make sure your pet has guinea pig pellets, grass hay, and fresh water in his cage at all times.

- Good treats for guinea pigs are: green leafy vegetables, apples, oranges, and grapes. DON'T feed your guinea pig cabbage, broccoli, iceberg lettuce, or potatoes.

- Provide a covered sleeping box inside the cage as well as safe things to chew (small pieces of untreated/unpainted wood or twigs that have not been sprayed with pesticide).

- Long-haired guinea pigs should be brushed daily. Short-haired guinea pigs would enjoy grooming, too!

Do you think a guinea pig is right for you? Great! Before buying one from a pet store, consider adopting a guinea pig from an animal shelter or from a rescue group. There are many waiting for a loving home just like yours!

For more information on how to help animals, go to
www.aspca.org/parents